Jonas Hanway

Virtue in Humble Life

Containing reflections on relative duties, particularly those of masters and servants.

Thoughts on the passions, prejudices, and tempers of mankind, drawn from real

characters. Fables applicable to the subjects.

Jonas Hanway

Virtue in Humble Life
Containing reflections on relative duties, particularly those of masters and servants. Thoughts on the passions, prejudices, and tempers of mankind, drawn from real characters. Fables applicable to the subjects.

ISBN/EAN: 9783744780438

Printed in Europe, USA, Canada, Australia, Japan

Cover: Foto ©Andreas Hilbeck / pixelio.de

More available books at **www.hansebooks.com**

He rushed against Horatius,
And smote with all his might.

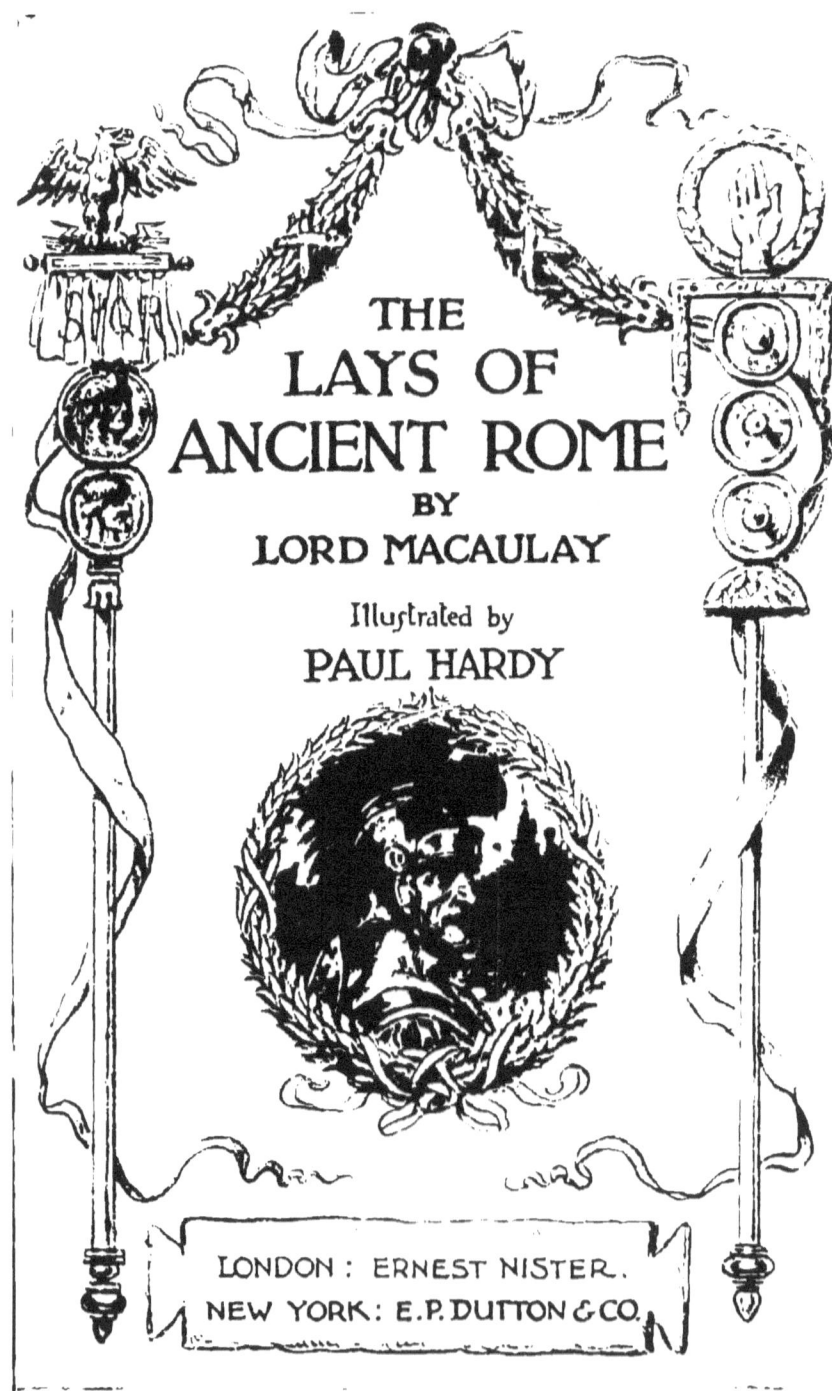

THE
LAYS OF
ANCIENT ROME

BY

LORD MACAULAY

Illustrated by

PAUL HARDY

LONDON : ERNEST NISTER.

NEW YORK : E.P. DUTTON & CO.

1861.

CONTENTS

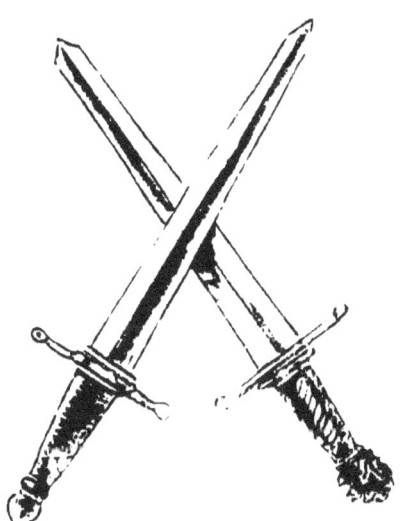

HORATIUS.

A LAY MADE ABOUT THE YEAR OF THE
CITY CCCLX.

I.

L ARS PORSENA of Clusium
    By the Nine Gods he swore
That the great house of Tarquin
    Should suffer wrong no more.
By the Nine Gods he swore it,
    And named a trysting day,
And bade his messengers ride forth,
East and west and south and north,
    To summon his array.

II.

East and west and south and north
  The messengers ride fast,
And tower and town and cottage
  Have heard the trumpet's blast.
Shame on the false Etruscan
  Who lingers in his home,
When Porsena of Clusium
  Is on the march for Rome.

III.

The horsemen and the footmen
  Are pouring in amain
From many a stately market-place;
  From many a fruitful plain;
From many a lonely hamlet,
  Which, hid by beech and pine,
Like an eagle's nest, hangs on the crest
  Of purple Apennine;

IV.

From lordly Volaterræ,
  Where scowls the far-famed hold
Piled by the hands of giants
  For godlike kings of old;
From seagirt Populonia,
  Whose sentinels descry
Sardinia's snowy mountain-tops
  Fringing the southern sky;

V.

From the proud mart of Pisæ,
  Queen of the western waves,
Where ride Massilia's triremes
  Heavy with fair-haired slaves;
From where sweet Clanis wanders
  Through corn and vines and flowers;
From where Cortona lifts to heaven
  Her diadem of towers.

VI.

Tall are the oaks whose acorns
  Drop in dark Auser's rill;
Fat are the stags that champ the boughs
  Of the Ciminian hill;
Beyond all streams Clitumnus
  Is to the herdsman dear;
Best of all pools the fowler loves
  The great Volsinian mere.

VII.

But now no stroke of woodman
  Is heard by Auser's rill;
No hunter tracks the stag's green path
  Up the Ciminian hill;
Unwatched along Clitumnus
  Grazes the milk-white steer;
Unharmed the water fowl may dip
  In the Volsinian mere.

VIII.

The harvests of Arretium,
   This year, old men shall reap,
This year, young boys in Umbro
   Shall plunge the struggling sheep;
And in the vats of Luna,
   This year, the must shall foam
Round the white feet of laughing girls
   Whose sires have marched to Rome.

IX.

There be thirty chosen prophets,
   The wisest of the land,
Who alway by Lars Porsena
   Both morn and evening stand:
Evening and morn the Thirty
   Have turned the verses o'er,
Traced from the right on linen white
   By mighty seers of yore.

X.

And with one voice the Thirty
Have their glad answer given:
"Go forth, go forth, Lars Porsena;
Go forth, beloved of Heaven;
Go, and return in glory
To Clusium's royal dome;
And hang round Nurscia's altars
The golden shields of Rome."

XI.

And now hath every city
Sent up her tale of men;
The foot are fourscore thousand,
The horse are thousands ten:
Before the gates of Sutrium
Is met the great array.
A proud man was Lars Porsena
Upon the trysting day.

XII.

For all the Etruscan armies
  Were ranged beneath his eye,
And many a banished Roman,
  And many a stout ally;
And with a mighty following
  To join the muster came
The Tusculan Mamilius,
  Prince of the Latian name.

XIII.

But by the yellow Tiber
  Was tumult and affright:
From all the spacious champaign
  To Rome men took their flight.
A mile around the city,
  The throng stopped up the ways;
A fearful sight it was to see
  Through two long nights and days

XIV.

For aged folks on crutches,
　　And women great with child,
And mothers sobbing over babes
　　That clung to them and smiled,
And sick men borne in litters
　　High on the necks of slaves,
And troops of sun-burned husbandmen
　　With reaping-hooks and staves,

XV.

And droves of mules and asses
   Laden with skins of wine,
And endless flocks of goats and sheep,
   And endless herds of kine,
And endless trains of waggons
   That creaked beneath the weight
Of corn-sacks and of household goods,
   Choked every roaring gate.

XVI.

Now, from the rock Tarpeian,
   Could the wan burghers spy
The line of blazing villages
   Red in the midnight sky.
The Fathers of the City,
   They sat all night and day,
For every hour some horseman came
   With tidings of dismay.

XVII.

To eastward and to westward
    Have spread the Tuscan bands;
Nor house, nor fence, nor dovecote
    In Crustumerium stands.
Verbenna down to Ostia
    Hath wasted all the plain;
Astur hath stormed Janiculum,
    And the stout guards are slain.

XVIII.

I wis, in all the Senate,
    There was no heart so bold,
But sore it ached and fast it beat,
    When that ill news was told.
Forthwith up rose the Consul,
    Up rose the Fathers all;
In haste they girded up their gowns,
    And hied them to the wall.

XIX.

They held a council standing
  Before the River-Gate;
Short time was there, ye well may guess,
  For musing or debate.

Out spake the Consul roundly:
  "The bridge must straight go down;
For, since Janiculum is lost,
  Nought else can save the town."

XX.

Just then a scout came flying,
　All wild with haste and fear;
"To arms! to arms! Sir Consul:
　Lars Porsena is here."
On the low hills to westward
　The Consul fixed his eye,
And saw the swarthy storm of dust
　Rise fast along the sky.

XXI.

And nearer fast and nearer
　Doth the red whirlwind come;
And louder still and still more loud,
From underneath that rolling cloud,
Is heard the trumpet's war-note proud,
　The trampling, and the hum.
And plainly and more plainly
　Now through the gloom appears,
Far to left and far to right,
In broken gleams of dark-blue light,

The long array of helmets bright,
The long array of spears.

XXII.

And plainly and more plainly,
 Above that glimmering line,
Now might ye see the banners
 Of twelve fair cities shine ;
But the banner of proud Clusium
 Was highest of them all,
The terror of the Umbrian,
 The terror of the Gaul.

XXIII.

And plainly and more plainly
 Now might the burghers know,
By port and vest, by horse and crest,
 Each warlike Lucumo.
There Cilnius of Arretium
 On his fleet roan was seen ;
And Astur of the four-fold shield,
Girt with the brand none else may wield,

Tolumnius with the belt of gold,
And dark Verbenna from the hold
  By reedy Thrasymene.

XXIV.

Fast by the royal standard,
  O'erlooking all the war,
Lars Porsena of Clusium
  Sat in his ivory car.
By the right wheel rode Mamilius,
  Prince of the Latian name;
And by the left false Sextus,
  That wrought the deed of shame.

XXV.

But when the face of Sextus
  Was seen among the foes,
A yell that rent the firmament
  From all the town arose.
On the house-tops was no woman
  But spat towards him and hissed,
No child but screamed out curses,
  And shook its little fist.

XXVI.

But the Consul's brow was sad,
  And the Consul's speech was low,
And darkly looked he at the wall,
  And darkly at the foe.

"Their van will be upon us
  Before the bridge goes down;
And if they once may win the bridge,
  What hope to save the town?"

XXVII.

Then out spake brave Horatius,
  The Captain of the Gate:
"To every man upon this earth
  Death cometh soon or late.
And how can man die better
  Than facing fearful odds,
For the ashes of his fathers,
  And the temples of his Gods,

XXVIII.

"And for the tender mother
  Who dandled him to rest,
And for the wife who nurses
  His baby at her breast,
And for the holy maidens
  Who feed the eternal flame,
To save them from false Sextus
  That wrought the deed of shame?

XXIX.

"Hew down the bridge, Sir Consul,
    With all the speed ye may;
I, with two more to help me,
    Will hold the foe in play.
In yon strait path a thousand
    May well be stopped by three.
Now who will stand on either hand,
    And keep the bridge with me?"

XXX.

Then out spake Spurius Lartius;
    A Ramnian proud was he:
"Lo, I will stand at thy right hand,
    And keep the bridge with thee."
And out spake strong Herminius;
    Of Titian blood was he:
"I will abide on thy left side,
    And keep the bridge with thee."

XXXI.

"Horatius," quoth the Consul,
    "As thou sayest, so let it be."
And straight against that great array
    Forth went the dauntless Three.
For Romans in Rome's quarrel
    Spared neither land nor gold,
Nor son nor wife, nor limb nor life,
    In the brave days of old.

XXXII.

Then none was for a party;
　　Then all were for the state;
Then the great man helped the poor,
　　And the poor man loved the great:
Then lands were fairly portioned;
　　Then spoils were fairly sold:
The Romans were like brothers
　　In the brave days of old.

XXXIII.

Now Roman is to Roman
　　More hateful than a foe
And the Tribunes beard the high,
　　And the Fathers grind the low.
As we wax hot in faction,
　　In battle we wax cold:
Wherefore men fight not as they fought
　　In the brave days of old.

XXXIV.

Now while the Three were tightening
  Their harness on their backs,
The Consul was the foremost man
  To take in hand an axe:
And Fathers mixed with Commons
  Seized hatchet, bar, and crow,
And smote upon the planks above,
  And loosed the props below.

XXXV.

Meanwhile the Tuscan army,
  Right glorious to behold,
Came flashing back the noonday light,
Rank behind rank, like surges bright
  Of a broad sea of gold.
Four hundred trumpets sounded
  A peal of warlike glee,
As that great host, with measured tread,

And spears advanced, and ensigns spread,
Rolled slowly towards the bridge's head,
Where stood the dauntless Three.

XXXVI.

The Three stood calm and silent,
    And looked upon the foes,
And a great shout of laughter
    From all the vanguard rose:
And forth three chiefs came spurring
    Before that deep array;
To earth they sprang, their swords they
        drew,
And lifted high their shields, and flew
    To win the narrow way:

XXXVII.

Aunus from green Tifernum,
    Lord of the Hill of Vines;
And Seius, whose eight hundred slaves
    Sicken in Ilva's mines;

And Picus, long to Clusium
  Vassal in peace and war,
Who led to fight his Umbrian powers
From that grey crag where, girt with towers,
The fortress of Nequinum lowers
  O'er the pale waves of Nar.

XXXVIII.

Stout Lartius hurled down Aunus
  Into the stream beneath:

Herminius struck at Seius,
  And clove him to the teeth:
At Picus brave Horatius
  Darted one fiery thrust;
And the proud Umbrian's gilded arms
  Clashed in the bloody dust.

XXXIX.

Then Ocnus of Falerii
  Rushed on the Roman Three:
And Lausulus of Urgo,
  The rover of the sea;
And Aruns of Volsinium,
  Who slew the great wild boar,
The great wild boar that had his den
Amidst the reeds of Cosa's fen,
And wasted fields, and slaughtered men,
  Along Albinia's shore.

XL.

Herminius smote down Aruns:
  Lartius laid Ocnus low:

Right to the heart of Lausulus
   Horatius sent a blow.
"Lie there," he cried, "fell pirate!
   No more, aghast and pale,
From Ostia's walls the crowd shall mark
The track of thy destroying bark.
No more Campania's hinds shall fly
To woods and caverns when they spy
   Thy thrice accursed sail."

XLI.

But now no sound of laughter
   Was heard among the foes.
A wild and wrathful clamour
   From all the vanguard rose.
Six spears' lengths from the entrance
   Halted that deep array,
And for a space no man came forth
   To win the narrow way.

XLII.

But hark! the cry is Astur:
   And lo! the ranks divide;

And the great Lord of Luna
  Comes with his stately stride.
Upon his ample shoulders
  Clangs loud the fourfold shield,
And in his hand he shakes the brand
  Which none but he can wield.

XLIII.

He smiled on those bold Romans
  A smile serene and high:
He eyed the flinching Tuscans,
  And scorn was in his eye.
Quoth he, "The she-wolf's litter
  Stand savagely at bay:
But will ye dare to follow,
  If Astur clears the way?

XLIV.

Then, whirling up his broadsword
  With both hands to the height,
He rushed against Horatius,
  And smote with all his might.

With shield and blade Horatius
  Right deftly turned the blow.
The blow, though turned,
                  came yet too nigh;
It missed his helm, but gashed his thigh:
The Tuscans raised a joyful cry
  To see the red blood flow.

XLV.

He reeled, and on Herminius
  He leaned one breathing-space,

Then, like a wild cat mad with wounds,
  Sprang right at Astur's face;
Through teeth, and skull, and helmet,
  So fierce a thrust he sped,
The good sword stood a hand-breadth out
  Behind the Tuscan's head.

XLVI.

And the great Lord of Luna
  Fell at that deadly stroke,
As falls on Mount Alvernus
  A thunder-smitten oak.
Far o'er the crashing forest
  The giant arms lie spread;
And the pale augurs, muttering low,
  Gaze on the blasted head.

XLVII.

On Astur's throat Horatius
  Right firmly pressed his heel,
And thrice and four times tugged amain,
  Ere he wrenched out the steel.

"And see," he cried, "the welcome,
  Fair guests, that waits you here!
What noble Lucumo comes next
  To taste our Roman cheer?"

XLVIII.

But at his haughty challenge
  A sullen murmur ran,
Mingled of wrath, and shame, and dread,
  Along that glittering van.
There lacked not men of prowess,
  Nor men of lordly race;
For all Etruria's noblest
  Were round the fatal place.

XLIX.

But all Etruria's noblest
  Felt their hearts sink to see
On the earth the bloody corpses,
  In the path the dauntless Three:
And, from the ghastly entrance
  Where those bold Romans stood,

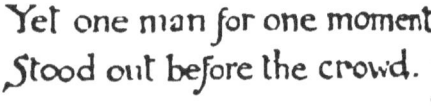

Yet one man for one moment
Stood out before the crowd.

All shrank, like boys who unaware,
Ranging the woods to start a hare,
Come to the mouth of the dark lair
Where, growling low, a fierce old bear
  Lies amidst bones and blood.

L.

Was none who would be foremost
  To lead such dire attack:
But those behind cried "Forward!"
  And those before cried "Back!"
And backward now and forward
  Wavers the deep array;
And on the tossing sea of steel,
To and fro the standards reel;
And the victorious trumpet-peal
  Dies fitfully away.

LI.

Yet one man for one moment
  Stood out before the crowd;

Well known was he to all the Three,
    And they gave him greeting loud,
"Now welcome, welcome, Sextus!
    Now welcome to thy home!
Why dost thou stay, and turn away?
    Here lies the road to Rome."

LII.

Thrice looked he at the city;
    Thrice looked he at the dead;
And thrice came on in fury,
    And thrice turned back in dread:
And, white with fear and hatred,
    Scowled at the narrow way
Where, wallowing in a pool of blood,
    The bravest Tuscans lay.

LIII.

But meanwhile axe and lever
    Have manfully been plied;
And now the bridge hangs tottering
    Above the boiling tide.

"Come back, come back, Horatius!"
Loud cried the Fathers all.
"Back, Lartius! back, Herminius!
Back, ere the ruin fall!"

LIV.

Back darted Spurius Lartius;
Herminius darted back:

And, as they passed, beneath their feet
　　They felt the timbers crack.
But when they turned their faces,
　　And on the farther shore
Saw brave Horatius stand alone,
　　They would have crossed once more

LV.

But with a crash like thunder
　　Fell every loosened beam,
And, like a dam, the mighty wreck
　　Lay right athwart the stream:
And a long shout of triumph
　　Rose from the walls of Rome,
As to the highest turret-tops
　　Was splashed the yellow foam.

LVI.

· And, like a horse unbroken
　　When first he feels the rein,
The furious river struggled hard,
　　And tossed his tawny mane,

And burst the curb, and bounded,
    Rejoicing to be free,
And whirling down, in fierce career,
Battlement, and plank, and pier,
    Rushed headlong to the sea.

LVII.

Alone stood brave Horatius,
    But constant still in mind;
Thrice thirty thousand foes before,
    And the broad flood behind.
"Down with him!" cried false Sextus,
    With a smile on his pale face.
"Now yield thee," cried Lars Porsena,
    "Now yield thee to our grace."

LVIII.

Round turned he, as not deigning
    Those craven ranks to see;
Nought spake he to Lars Porsena,
    To Sextus nought spake he;

But he saw on Palatinus
    The white porch of his home;
And he spake to the noble river
    That rolls by the towers of Rome.

LIX.

"Oh, Tiber! father Tiber!
    To whom the Romans pray,
A Roman's life, a Roman's arms,
    Take thou in charge this day!"
So he spake, and speaking sheathed,
    The good sword by his side
And with his harness on his back,
    Plunged headlong in the tide.

LX.

No sound of joy or sorrow
    Was heard from either bank;
But friends and foes in dumb surprise,
With parted lips and straining eyes,
    Stood gazing where he sank;
And when above the surges

They saw his crest appear,
All Rome sent forth a rapturous cry,
And even the ranks of Tuscany
    Could scarce forbear to cheer.

LXI.

But fiercely ran the current,
    Swollen high by months of rain:

And fast his blood was flowing;
  And he was sore in pain,
And heavy with his armour,
  And spent with changing blows:
And oft they thought him sinking,
  But still again he rose.

LXII.

Never, I ween, did swimmer,
  In such an evil case,
Struggle through such a raging flood
  Safe to the landing place:
But his limbs were borne up bravely
  By the brave heart within,
And our good father Tiber
  Bore bravely up his chin.

LXIII.

"Curse on him!" quoth false Sextus;
  "Will not the villain drown?
But for this stay, ere close of day
  We should have sacked the town!"

"Heaven help him!" quoth Lars Porsena,
   "And bring him safe to shore;
For such a gallant feat of arms
   Was never seen before."

LXIV.

And now he feels the bottom:
   Now on dry earth he stands;
Now round him throng the Fathers
   To press his gory hands;
And now, with shouts and clapping,
   And noise of weeping loud,
He enters through the River-Gate,
   Borne by the joyous crowd.

LXV.

They gave him of the corn-land,
   That was of public right,
As much as two strong oxen
   Could plough from morn till night,
And they made a molten image,
   And set it up on high,

And there it stands unto this day
    To witness if I lie.

LXVI.

It stands in the Comitium,
    Plain for all folk to see;
Horatius in his harness,
    Halting upon one knee:

And underneath is written,
  In letters all of gold,
How valiantly he kept the bridge
  In the brave days of old.

LXVII.

And still his name sounds stirring
  Unto the men of Rome,
As the trumpet-blast that cries to them
  To charge the Volscian home;
And wives still pray to Juno
  For boys with hearts as bold
As his who kept the bridge so well
  In the brave days of old.

LXVIII.

And in the nights of winter,
  When the cold north winds blow,
And the long howling of the wolves
  Is heard amidst the snow;
When round the lonely cottage
  Roars loud the tempest's din,

And the good logs of Algidus
  Roar louder yet within;

LXIX.

When the oldest cask is opened,
  And the largest lamp is lit;
When the chestnuts glow in the embers,
  And the kid turns on the spit;
When young and old in circle
  Around the firebrands close;
When the girls are weaving baskets,
  And the lads are shaping bows;

LXX.

When the goodman mends his armour,
  And trims his helmet's plume;
When the goodwife's shuttle merrily
  Goes flashing through the loom;
With weeping and with laughter
  Still is the story told,
How well Horatius kept the bridge
  In the brave days of old.

THE BATTLE
OF THE LAKE REGILLUS.

A LAY SUNG AT THE FEAST OF CASTOR AND
POLLUX, ON THE IDES OF QUINTILIS, IN THE
YEAR OF THE CITY CCCCLI.

I.

HO, trumpets, sound a war-note!
Ho, lictors, clear the way!
The Knights will ride, in all their pride,
Along the streets to-day.
To-day the doors and windows
Are hung with garlands all,
From Castor in the Forum,
To Mars without the wall.

Each Knight is robed in purple,
    With olive each is crowned;
A gallant war-horse under each
    Paws haughtily the ground.
While flows the Yellow River,
    While stands the Sacred Hill,
The proud Ides of Quintilis
    Shall have such honour still.
Gay are the Martian Kalends:
    December's Nones are gay:
But the proud Ides,
            when the squadron rides,
    Shall be Rome's whitest day.

II.

Unto the Great Twin Brethren
    We keep this solemn feast.
Swift, swift, the Great Twin Brethren
    Came spurring from the east.
They came o'er wild Parthenius
    Tossing in waves of pine,
O'er Cirrha's dome, o'er Adria's foam,
    O'er purple Apennine,

From where with flutes and dances
    Their ancient mansion rings,
In lordly Lacedæmon,
    The City of two kings,
To where, by Lake Regillus
    Under the Porcian height,
All in the lands of Tusculum,
    Was fought the glorious fight.

III.

Now on the place of slaughter
    Are cots and sheepfolds seen,

And rows of vines, and fields of wheat,
　And apple-orchards green;
The swine crush the big acorns
　That fall from Corne's oaks.
Upon the turf by the Fair Fount
　The reaper's pottage smokes.
The fisher baits his angle;
　The hunter twangs his bow;
Little they think on those strong limbs
　That moulder deep below.
Little they think how sternly
　That day the trumpets pealed;
How in the slippery swamp of blood
　Warrior and war-horse reeled:
How wolves came with fierce gallop,
　And crows on eager wings,
To tear the flesh of captains,
　And peck the eyes of kings:
How thick the dead lay scattered
　Under the Porcian height;
How through the gates of Tusculum
　Raved the wild stream of flight;

And how the Lake Regillus
  Bubbled with crimson foam,
What time the Thirty Cities
  Came forth to war with Rome.

IV.

But, Roman, when thou standest
  Upon that holy ground,
Look thou with heed on the dark rock
  That girds the dark lake round,
So shalt thou see a hoof-mark
  Stamped deep into the flint:
It was no hoof of mortal steed
  That made so strange a dint:
There to the Great Twin Brethren
  Vow thou thy vows, and pray
That they, in tempest and in fight,
  Will keep thy head alway.

V.

Since last the Great Twin Brethren
  Of mortal eyes were seen,

Have years gone by an hundred
And fourscore and thirteen.
That summer a Virginius
Was Consul first in place;

The second was stout Aulus,
Of the Posthumian race.
The Herald of the Latines
From Gabii came in state:

The Herald of the Latines
   Passed through Rome's Eastern Gate:
The Herald of the Latines
   Did in our Forum stand;
And there he did his office,
   A sceptre in his hand.

VI.

"Hear, Senators and people
   Of the good town of Rome,
The Thirty Cities charge you
   To bring the Tarquins home:
And if ye still be stubborn,
   To work the Tarquins wrong,
The Thirty Cities warn you,
   Look that your walls be strong."

VII.

Then spake the Consul Aulus,
   He spake a bitter jest:
"Once the jay sent a message
   Unto the eagle's nest:—

Now yield thou up thine eyrie
  Unto the carrion-kite,
Or come forth valiantly, and face
  The jays in deadly fight.—
Forth looked in wrath the eagle;
  And carrion-kite and jay,
Soon as they saw his beak and claw,
  Fled screaming far away."

VIII.

The Herald of the Latines
  Hath hied him back in state;
The Fathers of the City
  Are met in high debate.
Then spake the elder Consul,
  An ancient man and wise:
"Now hearken, Conscript Fathers,
  To that which I advise.
In seasons of great peril
  'Tis good that one bear sway;
Then choose we a Dictator,
  Whom all men shall obey.

Camerium knows how deeply
　The sword of Aulus bites,
And all our city calls him
　The man of seventy fights.
Then let him be Dictator
　For six months and no more,
And have a Master of the Knights,
　And axes twenty-four."

IX.

So Aulus was Dictator,
　The man of seventy fights;
He made Æbutius Elva
　His Master of the Knights.
On the third morn thereafter,
　At dawning of the day,
Did Aulus and Æbutius
　Set forth with their array.
Sempronius Atratinus
　Was left in charge at home
With boys, and with grey-headed men,
　To keep the walls of Rome.

Hard by the Lake Regillus
Our camp was pitched at night:
Eastward a mile the Latines lay,
Under the Porcian height.

Far over hill and valley
Their mighty host was spread;
And with their thousand watch-fires
The midnight sky was red.

X.

Up rose the golden morning
  Over the Porcian height,
The proud Ides of Quintilis
  Marked evermore with white.
Not without secret trouble
  Our bravest saw the foes;
For girt by threescore thousand spears,
  The thirty standards rose.
From every warlike city
  That boasts the Latian name,
Foredoomed to dogs and vultures,
  That gallant army came;
From Setia's purple vineyards,
  From Norba's ancient wall,
From the white streets of Tusculum,
  The proudest town of all;
From where the Witch's Fortress
  O'erhangs the dark blue seas;
From the still glassy lake that sleeps
  Beneath Aricia's trees

Those trees in whose dim shadow
    The ghastly priest doth reign,
The priest who slew the slayer,
    And shall himself be slain;
From the drear banks of Ufens,
    Where flights of marsh-fowl play,
And buffaloes lie wallowing
    Through the hot summer's day;
From the gigantic watch-towers,
    No work of earthly men,
Whence Cora's sentinels o'erlooked
    The never-ending fen;
From the Laurentian jungle,
    The wild hog's reedy home;
From the green steeps whence Anio leaps
    In floods of snow-white foam.

XI.

Aricia, Cora, Norba,
    Velitræ, with the might
Of Setia and of Tusculum,
    Were marshalled on the right:

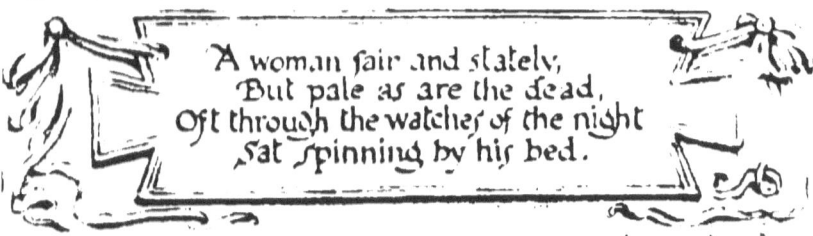

A woman fair and stately,
But pale as are the dead,
Oft through the watches of the night
Sat spinning by his bed.

The leader was Mamilius,
  Prince of the Latian name;
Upon his head a helmet
  Of red gold shone like flame:
High on a gallant charger
  Of dark-grey hue he rode:
Over his gilded armour
  A vest of purple flowed,
Woven in the land of sunrise
  By Syria's dark-browed daughters,
And by the sails of Carthage brought
  Far o'er the southern waters.

XII.

Lavinium and Laurentum
  Had on the left their post,
With all the banners of the marsh,
  And banners of the coast.
Their leader was false Sextus,
  That wrought the deed of shame:
With restless pace and haggard face
  To his last field he came.

Men said he saw strange visions
   Which none beside might see,
And that strange sounds were in his ears
   Which none might hear but he.
A woman, fair and stately,
   But pale as are the dead,
Oft through the watches of the night
   Sat spinning by his bed.
And as she plied the distaff,
   In a sweet voice and low,
She sang of great old houses,
   And fights fought long ago.
So spun she, and so sang she,
   Until the east was grey,
Then pointed to her bleeding breast,
   And shrieked, and fled away.

XIII.

But in the centre thickest
   Were ranged the shields of foes,
And from the centre loudest
   The cry of battle rose.

There Tibur marched and Pedum
　Beneath proud Tarquin's rule,
And Ferentinum of the rock,
　And Gabii of the pool.

There rode the Volscian succours:
　There, in a dark stern ring,
The Roman exiles gathered close
　Around the ancient king.

Though white as Mount Soracte,
　When winter nights are long,
His beard flowed down o'er mail and belt,
　His heart and hand were strong:
Under his hoary eyebrows
　Still flashed forth quenchless rage,
And, if the lance shook in his gripe,
　'Twas more with hate than age.
Close at his side was Titus
　On an Apulian steed,
Titus, the youngest Tarquin,
　Too good for such a breed.

XIV.

Now on each side the leaders
　Give signal for the charge;
And on each side the footmen
　Strode on with lance and targe;
And on each side the horsemen
　Struck their spurs deep in gore;
And front to front the armies
　Met with a mighty roar:

And under that great battle
The earth with blood was red;
And, like the Pomptine fog at morn,
The dust hung overhead;
And louder still and louder
Rose from the darkened field
The braying of the war-horns,
The clang of sword and shield,
The rush of squadrons sweeping
Like whirlwinds o'er the plain,
The shouting of the slayers,
And screeching of the slain.

XV.

False Sextus rode out foremost;
His look was high and bold;
His corselet was of bison's hide,
Plated with steel and gold.
As glares the famished eagle
From the Digentian rock
On a choice lamb that bounds alone
Before Bandusia's flock,

Herminius glared on Sextus,
  And came with eagle speed,
Herminius on black Auster,
  Brave champion on brave steed:
In his right hand the broadsword
  That kept the bridge so well,
And on his helm the crown he won
  When proud Fidenæ fell.
Woe to the maid whose lover
  Shall cross his path to-day!
False Sextus saw, and trembled,
  And turned, and fled away.
As turns, as flies, the woodman
  In the Calabrian brake,
When through the reeds
              gleams the round eye
  Of that fell speckled snake;
So turned, so fled, false Sextus
  And hid him in the rear,
Behind the dark Lavinian ranks,
  Bristling with crest and spear.

XVI.

But far to north Æbutius,
    The Master of the Knights,
Gave Tubero of Norba
    To feed the Porcian kites.
Next under those red horse-hoofs
    Flaccus of Setia lay;
Better had he been pruning
    Among his elms that day.
Mamilius saw the slaughter,
    And tossed his golden crest,
And towards the Master of the Knights
    Through the thick battle pressed.
Æbutius smote Mamilius
    So fiercely on the shield
That the great lord of Tusculum
    Well nigh rolled on the field.
Mamilius smote Æbutius,
    With a good aim and true,
Just where the neck and shoulder join,
    And pierced him through
            and through;

And brave Æbutius Elva
　　Fell swooning to the ground;
But a thick wall of bucklers
　　Encompassed him around.
His clients from the battle
　　Bare him some little space,
And filled a helm from the dark lake,
　　And bathed his brow and face;
And when at last he opened
　　His swimming eyes to light,
Men say, the earliest word he spake
　　Was, "Friends, how goes the fight?"

XVII.

But meanwhile in the centre
　　Great deeds of arms were wrought;
There Aulus the Dictator
　　And there Valerius fought.
Aulus with his good broadsword
　　A bloody passage cleared
To where, amidst the thickest foes,
　　He saw the long white beard.

Flat lighted that good broadsword
    Upon proud Tarquin's head.
He dropped the lance:
            he dropped the reins:
I le fell as fall the dead.
Down Aulus springs to slay him,
    With eyes like coals of fire;
But faster Titus hath sprung down,
    And hath bestrode his sire.

Latian captains, Roman knights,
  Fast down to earth they spring,
And hand to hand they fight on foot
  Around the ancient king.
First Titus gave tall Cæso
  A death wound in the face;
Tall Cæso was the bravest man
  Of the brave Fabian race:
Aulus slew Rex of Gabii,
  The priest of Juno's shrine;
Valerius smote down Julius,
  Of Rome's great Julian line;
Julius, who left his mansion
  High on the Velian hill,
And through all turns of weal and woe
  Followed proud Tarquin still.
Now right across proud Tarquin
  A corpse was Julius laid;
And Titus groaned with rage and grief,
  And at Valerius made.
Valerius struck at Titus,
  And lopped off half his crest;

But Titus stabbed Valerius
  A span deep in the breast.
Like a mast snapped by the tempest,
  Valerius reeled and fell.
Ah! woe is me for the good house
  That loves the people well!
Then shouted loud the Latines:
  And with one rush they bore
The struggling Romans backward
  Three lances' length and more:
And up they took proud Tarquin,
  And laid him on a shield,
And four strong yeomen bare him,
  Still senseless, from the field.

XVIII.

But fiercer grew the fighting
  Around Valerius dead:
For Titus dragged him by the foot,
  And Aulus by the head.
"On, Latines, on!" quoth Titus.
  "See how the rebels fly!"

"Romans, stand firm!" quoth Aulus.
    "And win this fight or die!
They must not give Valerius
    To raven and to kite;
For aye Valerius loathed the wrong,
    And aye upheld the right:
And for your wives and babies
    In the front rank he fell.
Now play the men for the good house
    That loves the people well!"

XIX.

Then tenfold round the body
    The roar of battle rose,
Like the roar of a burning forest,
    When a strong north wind blows.
Now backward, and now forward,
    Rocked furiously the fray,
Till none could see Valerius,
    And none wist where he lay.
For shivered arms and ensigns
    Were heaped there in a mound,

And corpses stiff, and dying men
That writhed and gnawed the ground;
And wounded horses kicking,
And snorting purple foam :
Right well did such a couch befit
A Consular of Rome.

XX.

But north looked the Dictator;
North looked he long and hard;
And spake to Caius Cossus,
The Captain of his Guard:
"Caius, of all the Romans
Thou hast the keenest sight;
Say, what through yonder storm of dust
Comes from the Latian right?"

XXI.

Then answered Caius Cossus,
"I see an evil sight;
The banner of proud Tusculum
Comes from the Latian right;

I see the plumèd horsemen;
  And far before the rest
I see the dark-grey charger,
  I see the purple vest;
I see the golden helmet
  That shines far off like flame;
So ever rides Mamilius,
  Prince of the Latian name."

XXII.

"Now hearken, Caius Cossus:
  Spring on thy horse's back;
Ride as the wolves of Apennine
  Were all upon thy track;
Haste to our southward battle:
  And never draw thy rein
Until thou find Herminius,
  And bid him come amain."

XXIII.

So Aulus spake, and turned him
  Again to that fierce strife;

And Caius Cossus mounted,
    And rode for death and life.
Loud clanged beneath his horse-hoofs
    The helmets of the dead,
And many a curdling pool of blood
    Splashed him from heel to head.
So came he far to southward,
    Where fought the Roman host,
Against the banners of the marsh
    And banners of the coast.
Like corn before the sickle
    The stout Lavinians fell,
Beneath the edge of the true sword
    That kept the bridge so well.

XXIV.

"Herminius! Aulus greets thee;
    He bids thee come with speed,
To help our central battle,
    For sore is there our need.
There wars the youngest Tarquin,
    And there the Crest of Flame,

The Tusculan Mamilius,
   Prince of the Latian name.
Valerius hath fallen fighting
   In front of our array:
And Aulus of the seventy fields
   Alone upholds the day."

XXV.

Herminius beat his bosom:
   But never a word he spake.

He clapped his hand on Auster's mane;
  He gave the reins a shake.
Away, away went Auster,
  Like an arrow from the bow:
Black Auster was the fleetest steed
  From Aufidus to Po.

XXVI.

Right glad were all the Romans
  Who, in that hour of dread,
Against great odds bare up the war
  Around Valerius dead,
When from the south the cheering
  Rose with a mighty swell;
"Herminius comes, Herminius,
  Who kept the bridge so well!"

XXVII.

Mamilius spied Herminius,
  And dashed across the way.
"Herminius! I have sought thee
  Through many a bloody day.

One of us two, Herminius,
    Shall never more go home.
I will lay on for Tusculum,
    And lay thou on for Rome!"

XXVIII.

All round them paused the battle.
    While met in mortal fray
The Roman and the Tusculan,
    The horses black and grey.
Herminius smote Mamilius
    Through breast-plate
                and through breast;
And fast flowed out the purple blood
    Over the purple vest.
Mamilius smote Herminius
    Through head-piece
                and through head;
And side by side those chiefs of pride
    Together fell down dead.
Down fell they dead together
    In a great lake of gore;

And still stood all who saw them fall
While men might count a score.

XXIX.

Fast, fast, with heels wild spurning.
The dark-grey charger fled:
He burst through ranks of fighting men.
He sprang o'er heaps of dead.
His bridle far out-streaming,
His flanks all blood and foam,
He sought the southern mountains,
The mountains of his home.
The pass was steep and rugged,
The wolves they howled and whined;
But he ran like a whirlwind up the pass.
And he left the wolves behind.
Through many a startled hamlet
Thundered his flying feet;
He rushed through the gate of Tusculum,
He rushed up the long white street;
He rushed by tower and temple,
And paused not from his race

Till he stood before his master's door
   In the stately market-place.
And straightway round him gathered
   A pale and trembling crowd,
And when they knew him, cries of rage
   Brake forth, and wailing loud,
And women rent their tresses
   For their great prince's fall;
And old men girt on their old swords,
   And went to man the wall.

XXX.

But, like a graven image,
   Black Auster kept his place,
And ever wistfully he looked
   Into his master's face.
The raven mane that daily,
   With pats and fond caresses,
The young Herminia washed and combed
   And twined in even tresses,
And decked with coloured ribands
   From her own gay attire,

Hung sadly o'er her father's corpse
   In carnage and in mire.
Forth with a shout sprang Titus,
   And seized black Auster's rein.
Then Aulus sware a fearful oath,
   And ran at him amain.
"The furies of thy brother
   With me and mine abide,
If one of your accursed house
   Upon black Auster ride!"
As on an Alpine watch-tower
   From heaven comes down the flame,
Full on the neck of Titus
   The blade of Aulus came:
And out the red blood spouted,
   In a wide arch and tall,
As spouts a fountain in the court
   Of some rich Capuan's hall.
The knees of all the Latines
   Were loosened with dismay
When dead, on dead Herminius,
   The bravest Tarquin lay.

XXXI.

And Aulus the Dictator
  Stroked Auster's raven mane,
With heed he looked unto the girths,
  With heed unto the rein.
"Now bear me well, black Auster,
  Into yon thick array;
And thou and I will have revenge
  For thy good lord this day."

XXXII.

So spake he; and was buckling
   Tighter black Auster's band,
When he was aware of a princely pair
   That rode at his right hand.
So like they were, no mortal
   Might one from other know:
White as snow their armour was:
   Their steeds were white as snow.
Never on earthly anvil
   Did such rare armour gleam;
And never did such gallant steeds
   Drink of an earthly stream.

XXXIII.

And all who saw them trembled,
   And pale grew every cheek;
And Aulus the Dictator
   Scarce gathered voice to speak.
"Say by what name men call you?
   What city is your home?

And wherefore ride ye in such guise
Before the ranks of Rome?"

XXXIV.

"By many names men call us;
In many lands we dwell:
Well Samothracia knows us;
Cyrene knows us well.
Our house in gay Tarentum
Is hung each morn with flowers:
High o'er the mast of Syracuse
Our marble portal towers;
But by the proud Eurotas
Is our dear native home;
And for the right we come to fight
Before the ranks of Rome."

XXXV.

So answered those strange horsemen,
And each couched low his spear;
And forthwith all the ranks of Rome
Were bold, and of good cheer;

"The gods who live for ever
Are on our side to-day."

And on the thirty armies
  Came wonder and affright,
And Ardea wavered on the left,
  And Cora on the right.
"Rome to the charge!" cried Aulus;
  "The foe begins to yield!
Charge for the hearth of Vesta!
  Charge for the Golden Shield!
Let no man stop to plunder,
  But slay, and slay, and slay;
The gods who live for ever
  Are on our side to-day."

XXXVI.

Then the fierce trumpet-flourish
  From earth to heaven arose.
The kites know well the long stern swell
  That bids the Romans close.
Then the good sword of Aulus
  Was lifted up to slay:
Then, like a crag down Apennine,
  Rushed Auster through the fray.

But under those strange horsemen
    Still thicker lay the slain;
And after those strange horses
    Black Auster toiled in vain.
Behind them Rome's long battle
    Came rolling on the foe,
Ensigns dancing wild above,
    Blades all in line below.
So comes the Po in flood-time
    Upon the Celtic plain:
So comes the squall, blacker than night,
    Upon the Adrian main.
Now, by our Sire Quirinus,
    It was a goodly sight
To see the thirty standards
    Swept down the tide of flight.
So flies the spray of Adria
    When the black squall doth blow,
So corn-sheaves in the flood-time
    Spin down the whirling Po.
False Sextus to the mountains
    Turned first his horse's head;

And fast fled Ferentinum,
    And fast Lanuvium fled.
The horsemen of Nomentum
    Spurred hard out of the fray;
The footmen of Velitræ
    Threw shield and spear away.
And underfoot was trampled,
    Amidst the mud and gore,

The banner of proud Tusculum,
   That never stooped before:
And down went Flavius Faustus,
   Who led his stately ranks
From where the apple blossoms wave
   On Anio's echoing banks,
And Tullus of Arpinum,
   Chief of the Volscian aids,
And Metius with the long fair curls,
   The love of Anxur's maids,
And the white head of Vulso,
   The great Arician seer,
And Nepos of Laurentum,
   The hunter of the deer;
And in the back false Sextus
   Felt the good Roman steel,
And wriggling in the dust he died
   Like a worm beneath the wheel.
And fliers and pursuers
   Were mingled in a mass;
And far away the battle
   Went roaring through the pass.

XXXVII.

Sempronius Atratinus
    Sate in the Eastern Gate,
Beside him were three Fathers,
    Each in his chair of state;
Fabius, whose nine stout grandsons
    That day were in the field,
And Manlius, eldest of the Twelve
    Who kept the Golden Shield;
And Sergius, the High Pontiff,
    For wisdom far renowned;
In all Etruria's colleges
    Was no such Pontiff found.
And all around the portal,
    And high above the wall,
Stood a great throng of people,
    But sad and silent all;
Young lads, and stooping elders
    That might not bear the mail,
Matrons with lips that quivered,
    And maids with faces pale.

Since the first gleam of daylight,
　Sempronius had not ceased
To listen for the rushing
　Of horse-hoofs from the east.
The mist of eve was rising,
　The sun was hastening down,
When he was aware of a princely pair
　Fast pricking towards the town.
So like they were, man never
　Saw twins so like before;
Red with gore their armour was,
　Their steeds were red with gore.

XXXVIII.

"Hail to the great Asylum!
　Hail to the hill-tops seven!
Hail to the fire that burns for aye,
　And the shield that
　　　　　　fell from heaven!
This day, by Lake Regillus,
　Under the Porcian height,

All in the lands of Tusculum
  Was fought a glorious fight.
To-morrow your Dictator
  Shall bring in triumph home
The spoils of thirty cities
  To deck the shrines of Rome!"

XXXIX.

Then burst from that great concourse
  A shout that shook the towers,
And some ran north,
            and some ran south,
  Crying, "The day is ours!"
But on rode these strange horsemen,
  With slow and lordly pace;
And none who saw their bearing
  Durst ask their name or race.
On rode they to the Forum,
  While laurel boughs and flowers,
From house-tops and from windows,
  Fell on their crests in showers.

When they drew nigh to Vesta,
   They vaulted down amain,
And washed their horses in the well
   That springs by Vesta's fane.
And straight again they mounted,
   And rode to Vesta's door;
Then, like a blast,
          away they passed,
   And no man saw them more.

XL.

And all the people trembled,
   And pale grew every cheek;
And Sergius the High Pontiff
   Alone found voice to speak:
"The gods who live for ever
   Have fought for Rome to-day!
These be the Great Twin Brethren
   To whom the Dorians pray.
Back comes the chief in triumph,
   Who, in the hour of fight,

Hath seen the Great Twin Brethren
    In harness on his right.
Safe comes the ship to haven,
    Through billows and through gales,

If once the Great Twin Brethren
    Sit shining on the sails.
Wherefore they washed their horses
    In Vesta's holy well,

Wherefore they rode to Vesta's door,
   I know, but may not tell.
Here, hard by Vesta's Temple,
   Build we a stately dome
Unto the Great Twin Brethren
   Who fought so well for Rome.
And when the months returning
   Bring back this day of fight,
The proud Ides of Quintilis,
   Marked evermore with white,
Unto the Great Twin Brethren
   Let all the people throng,
With chaplets and with offerings,
   With music and with song;
And let the doors and windows
   Be hung with garlands all,
And let the Knights be summoned
   To Mars without the wall;
Thence let them ride in purple
   With joyous trumpet-sound,
Each mounted on his war-horse,
   And each with olive crowned;

And pass in solemn order
    Before the sacred dome,
Where dwell the Great Twin Brethren
    Who fought so well for Rome!"

VIRGINIA

FRAGMENTS OF A LAY SUNG IN THE FORUM
ON THE DAY WHEREON LUCIUS SEXTIUS
SEXTINUS LATERANUS AND CAIUS LICINIUS
CALVUS STOLO WERE ELECTED TRIBUNES OF
THE COMMONS THE FIFTH TIME, IN THE YEAR
OF THE CITY CCCLXXXII.

YE good men of the Commons,
   with loving hearts and true,
Who stand by the bold Tribunes
   that still have stood by you,
Come, make a circle round me,
   and mark my tale with care,
A tale of what Rome once hath borne,
   of what Rome yet may bear.

This is no Grecian fable,
       of fountains running wine,
Of maids with snaky tresses,
       or sailors turned to swine.
Here, in this very Forum,
       under the noonday sun,
In sight of all the people,
       the bloody deed was done.
Old men still creep among
       us who saw that fearful day,
Just seventy years and seven ago,
       when the wicked Ten bare sway.
Of all the wicked Ten still
       the names are held accursed,
And of all the wicked Ten
       Appius Claudius was the worst.
He stalked along the Forum
       like King Tarquin in his pride:
Twelve axes waited on him,
       six marching on a side;

The townsmen shrank to right and left,
        and eyed askance with fear
His lowering brow, his curling mouth,
        which always seemed to sneer:
That brow of hate, that mouth of scorn,
        marks all the kindred still;
For never was there Claudius yet
        but wished the Commons ill:
Nor lacks he fit attendance;
        for close behind his heels,
With outstretched chin and crouching pace,
        the client Marcus steals,
His loins girt up to run with speed,
        be the errand what it may,
And the smile flickering on his cheek,
        for aught his lord may say,
Such varlets pimp and jest for hire
        among the lying Greeks:
Such varlets still are paid to hoot
        when brave Licinius speaks.

Where'er ye shed the honey,
   the buzzing flies will crowd;
Where'er ye fling the carrion,
   the raven's croak is loud;
Where'er down Tiber garbage floats,
   the greedy pike ye see;
And wheresoe'er such lord is found,
   such client still will be.
Just then, as through one cloudless
   chink in a black stormy sky
Shines out the dewy morning star,
   a fair young girl came by,
With her small tablets in her hand,
   and her satchel on her arm,
Home she went bounding from the school,
   nor dreamed of shame or harm;
And past those dreaded
   axes she innocently ran,
With bright, frank brow that had not
   learned to blush at gaze of man;

And up the Sacred Street she turned,
and, as she danced along,
She warbled gaily to herself
lines of the good old song,

How for a sport the princes
came spurring from the camp,
And found Lucrece, combing the fleece,
under the midnight lamp.

The maiden sang as sings the lark,
        when up he darts his flight
From his nest in the green April corn,
        to meet the morning light;
And Appius heard her sweet young voice,
        and saw her sweet young face,
And loved her with the accursèd
        love of his accursèd race,
And all along the Forum,
        and up the Sacred Street,
His vulture eye pursued the trip
        of those small glancing feet.

    *   *   *   *   *

Over the Alban mountains
        the light of morning broke;
From all the roofs of the Seven Hills
        curled the thin wreaths of smoke:
The city gates were opened;
        the Forum all alive

With buyers and with sellers

   was humming like a hive:
Blithely on brass and timber

   the craftsman's stroke was ringing,
And blithely o'er her panniers

   the market girl was singing,
And blithely young Virginia

   came smiling from her home:
Ah! woe for young Virginia,

   the sweetest maid in Rome!
With her small tablets in her hand,

   and her satchel on her arm,
Forth she went bounding to the school,

   nor dreamed of shame or harm.
She crossed the Forum shining

   with stalls in alleys gay,
And just had reached the very

   spot whereon I stand this day,
When up the varlet Marcus came;

   not such as when erewhile

Home she went bounding
from the school, nor
dreamed of shame or harm.

He crouched behind his patron's heels
      with the true client smile:
He came with lowering forehead,
      swollen features, and clenched fist,
And strode across Virginia's path,
      and caught her by the wrist.
Hard strove the frighted maiden,
      and screamed with look aghast;
And at her scream from right and left
      the folk came running fast;
The money-changer Crispus,
      with his thin silver hairs,
And Hanno from the stately booth
      glittering with Punic wares,
And the strong smith Muræna,
      grasping a half-forged brand,
And Volero the flesher,
      his cleaver in his hand.
All came in wrath and wonder;
      for all knew that fair child;

And, as she passed them twice a day,
          all kissed their hands and smiled;
And the strong smith Muræna
          gave Marcus such a blow,
The caitiff reeled three paces back,
          and let the maiden go.
Yet glared he fiercely round him,
          and growled in harsh, fell tone,
"She's mine, and I will have her:
          I seek but for mine own:
She is my slave, born in my house,
          and stolen away and sold,
The year of the sore sickness,
          ere she was twelve hours old.
'Twas in the sad September,
          the month of wail and fright,
Two augurs were borne forth that morn;
          the Consul died ere night.
I wait on Appius Claudius,
          I waited on his sire;

Let him who works the client

      wrong beware the patron's ire!"

  So spake the varlet Marcus;

        and dread and silence came

On all the people at the sound

      of the great Claudian name.

For then there was no Tribune

      to speak the word of might,

Which makes the rich man tremble,

      and guards the poor man's right.

There was no brave Licinius,

      no honest Sextius then;

But all the city, in great fear,

      obeyed the wicked Ten.

Yet ere the varlet Marcus again

      might seize the maid,

Who clung tight to Muræna's skirt,

      and sobbed, and shrieked for aid,

Forth through the throng of gazers

      the young Icilius pressed,

And stamped his foot, and rent his gown,

      and smote upon his breast,

And sprang upon that column

        by many a minstrel sung,

Whereon three mouldering helmets,

      three rusting swords, are hung,

And beckoned to the people,

      and in bold voice and clear

Poured thick and fast the burning words

    which tyrants quake to hear.

"Now, by your children's cradles,

    now by your fathers' graves,

Be men to-day, Quirites,

    or be for ever slaves!

For this did Servius give us laws?

    For this did Lucrece bleed?

For this was the great vengeance

    wrought on Tarquin's evil seed?

For this did those false sons make

    red the axes of their sire?

For this did Scævola's right hand

    hiss in the Tuscan fire?

Shall the vile fox-earth awe the race

    that stormed the lion's den?

Shall we, who could not brook one lord,

    crouch to the wicked Ten?

Oh, for that ancient spirit

    which curbed the Senate's will!

Oh, for the tents which in old time
                whitened the Sacred Hill!
In those brave days our fathers
                stood firmly side by side;
They faced the Marcian fury;
                they tamed the Fabian pride:
They drove the fiercest Quinctius
                an outcast forth from Rome:
They sent the haughtiest Claudius
                with shivered fasces home.
But what their care bequeathed
                us our madness flung away:
All the ripe fruit of threescore
                years was blighted in a day.
Exult, ye proud Patricians!
                The hard-fought fight is o'er.
We strove for honours -'twas in vain:
                for freedom—'tis no more.
No crier to the polling summons
                the eager throng:

No Tribune breathes the word of might
   that guards the weak from wrong.
Our very hearts, that were so high,
   sink down beneath your will.
Riches, and lands, and power, and state--
   ye have them:—keep them still
Still keep the holy fillets;
   still keep the purple gown,
The axes, and the curule chair,
   the car, and laurel crown:
Still press us for your cohorts, and,
   when the fight is done,
Still fill your garners from the soil
   which our good swords have won.
Still, like a spreading ulcer,
   which leech-craft may not cure,
Let your foul usance eat away
   the substance of the poor.
Still let your haggard debtors bear
   all their fathers bore;

Still let your dens of torment
                be noisome as of yore:
No fire when Tiber freezes;
                no air in dog-star heat:
And store of rods for free-born backs,
                and holes for free-born feet.
Heap heavier still the fetters;
                bar closer still the grate;
Patient as sheep we yield
                us up unto your cruel hate.
But, by the Shades beneath us,
                and by the Gods above,
Add not unto your cruel hate
                your yet more cruel love!
Have ye not graceful ladies,
                whose spotless lineage springs
From Consuls, and High Pontiffs,
                and ancient Alban kings?
Ladies, who deign not on our paths
                to set their tender feet,

Who from their cars look down with
          scorn upon the wondering street,
Who in Corinthian mirrors their
              own proud smiles behold,

And breathe of Capuan odours,
          and shine with Spanish gold?
Then leave the poor Plebeian
             his single tie to life—

The sweet, sweet love of daughter,
        of sister and of wife,
The gentle speech, the balm for all
        that his vexed soul endures,
The kiss, in which he half forgets even
        such a yoke as yours.
Still let the maiden's beauty swell
        the father's breast with pride;
Still let the bridegroom's arms infold
        an unpolluted bride.
Spare us the inexpiable wrong,
        the unutterable shame,
That turns the coward's heart to steel,
        the sluggard's blood to flame,
Lest, when our latest hope is fled,
        ye taste of our despair,
And learn by proof, in some wild hour,
        how much the wretched dare."

          *   *

Straightway Virginius led the maid
               a little space aside,
To where the reeking shambles stood,
               piled up with horn and hide,
Close to yon low dark archway,
               where, in a crimson flood,
Leaps down to the great sewer
               the gurgling stream of blood,
Hard by, a flesher on a block
               had laid his whittle down:
Virginius caught the whittle up,
               and hid it in his gown.
And then his eyes grew very dim,
               and his throat began to swell,
And in a hoarse, changed voice he spake.
    "Farewell, sweet child!   Farewell!
Oh! how I loved my darling!
               Though stern I sometimes be,
To thee, thou know'st I was not so.
               Who could be so to thee?

And how my darling loved me!
        How glad she was to hear
My footstep on the threshold when
        I came back last year!
And how she danced with pleasure
        to see my civic crown,
And took my sword, and hung it up,
        and brought me forth my gown!
Now, all those things are over—yes,
        all thy pretty ways,
Thy needlework, thy prattle,
        thy snatches of old lays:
And none will grieve when I go forth,
        or smile when I return,
Or watch beside the old man's bed,
        or weep upon his urn.
The house that was the happiest
        within the Roman walls,
The house that envied not the wealth
        of Capua's marble halls,

Now, for the brightness of thy smile,
    must have eternal gloom.
And for the music of thy voice,
    the silence of the tomb.
The time is come. See how he points
    his eager hand this way!
See how his eyes gloat on thy grief,
    like a kite's upon the prey!

With all his wit, he little deems,
        that, spurned, betrayed, bereft,
The father hath in his despair
        one fearful refuge left.
He little deems that in this hand
        I clutch what still can save
Thy gentle youth from taunts and blows,
        the portion of the slave;
Yea, and from nameless evil,
        that passeth taunt and blow—
Foul outrage which thou knowest not,
        which thou shalt never know.
Then clasp me round the neck once more,
        and give me one more kiss;
And now, mine own dear little girl,
        there is no way but this."
With that he lifted high the steel,
        and smote her in the side,
And in her blood she sank to earth,
        and with one sob she died.

Then, for a little moment,
          all people held their breath;
And through the crowded Forum
          was stillness as of death;
And in another moment brake
          forth from one and all
A cry as if the Volscians
          were coming o'er the wall.
Some with averted faces
          shrieking fled home amain;
Some ran to call a leech; and some
          ran to lift the slain:
Some felt her lips and little wrist,
          if life might there be found;
And some tore up their garments fast,
          and strove to stanch the wound.
In vain they ran, and felt, and stanched;
          for never truer blow
That good right arm had dealt
          in fight against a Volscian foe.

When Appius Claudius saw that deed,
          he shuddered and sank down,
And hid his face some little space
          with the corner of his gown,

Till, with white lips and bloodshot eyes,
          Virginius tottered nigh,
And stood before the judgment-seat,
          and held the knife on high.

"Oh! dwellers in the nether gloom,
    avengers of the slain,
By this dear blood I cry to you,
    do right between us twain;
And even as Appius Claudius
    hath dealt by me and mine,
Deal you by Appius Claudius
    and all the Claudian line!"
So spake the slayer of his child,
    and turned, and went his way;
But first he cast one haggard
    glance to where the body lay,
And writhed, and groaned a fearful groan,
    and then, with steadfast feet,
Strode right across the market-place
    unto the Sacred Street.
Then up sprang Appius Claudius:
    "Stop him; alive or dead!
Ten thousand pounds of copper
    to the man who brings his head."

He looked upon his clients;
> but none would work his will.
He looked upon his lictors;
> but they trembled, and stood still.
And, as Virginius through the press
> his way in silence cleft,
Ever the mighty multitude
> fell back to right and left.
And he hath passed in safety
> unto his woeful home,
And there ta'en horse to tell the camp
> what deeds are done in Rome.
By this the flood of people
> was swollen from every side,
And streets and porches round were
> filled with that o'erflowing tide;
And close around the body
> gathered a little train
Of them that were the nearest
> and dearest to the slain.

They brought a bier, and hung it with
                many a cypress crown,
And gently they uplifted her,
                and gently laid her down.
The face of Appius Claudius wore
                the Claudian scowl and sneer,
And in the Claudian note he cried,
                "What doth this rabble here?
Have they no crafts to mind at home,
                that hitherward they stray?
Ho! lictors, clear the market-place,
                and fetch the corpse away!"
The voice of grief and fury till
                then had not been loud;
But a deep sullen murmur
                wandered among the crowd,
Like the moaning noise that goes
                before the whirlwind on the deep,
Or the growl of a fierce watch-dog
                but half aroused from sleep.

But when the lictors at that word,
            tall yeomen all and strong,
Each with his axe and sheaf of twigs,
            went down into the throng,
Those old men say, who saw that day
            of sorrow and of sin,
That in the Roman Forum
            was never such a din.
The wailing, hooting, cursing,
            the howls of grief and hate,
Were heard beyond the Pincian Hill,
            beyond the Latin Gate.
But close around the body,
            where stood the little train
Of them that were the nearest
            and dearest to the slain,
No cries were there, but teeth set fast,
            low whispers and black frowns,
And breaking up of benches,
            and girding up o gowns.

'Twas well the lictors might not pierce
> to where the maiden lay,
Else surely had they been all twelve
> torn limb from limb that day.

Right glad they were to struggle back,
> blood streaming from their heads,
With axes all in splinters,
> and raiment all in shreds.

Then Appius Claudius gnawed his lip,
        and the blood left his cheek;
And thrice he beckoned with his hand,
        and thrice he strove to speak;
And thrice the tossing Forum
          set up a frightful yell;
"See, see, thou dog! what thou hast done;
        and hide thy shame in hell!
Thou that wouldst make our maidens
      slaves must first make slaves of men.
Tribunes!   Hurrah for Tribunes!
        Down with the wicked Ten!"
And straightway, thick as hailstones,
        came whizzing through the air
Pebbles, and bricks, and potsherds,
        all round the curule chair:
And upon Appius Claudius
        great fear and trembling came;
For never was a Claudius
      yet brave against aught but shame.

Though the great houses love us not,
            we own, to do them right,
That the great houses, all save one,
            have borne them well in fight.
Still Caius of Corioli,
            his triumphs and his wrongs,
His vengeance and his mercy,
            live in our camp-fire songs
Beneath the yoke of Furius
            oft have Gaul and Tuscan bowed;
And Rome may bear the pride
            of him of whom herself is proud.
But evermore a Claudius
            shrinks from a stricken field,
And changes colour like a maid
            at sight of sword and shield.
The Claudian triumphs all were
            won within the city towers:
The Claudian yoke was never
            pressed on any necks but ours.

A Cossus, like a wild cat,

            springs ever at the face;

A Fabius rushes like a boar

            against the shouting chase;

But the vile Claudian litter,

            raging with currish spite,

Still yelps and snaps at those who run,

            still runs from those who smite.

So now 'twas seen of Appius.

      When stones began to fly.
He shook, and crouched, and wrung

      his hands, and smote upon his thigh.
"Kind clients, honest lictors,

      stand by me in this fray!
Must I be torn in pieces?

      Home, home, the nearest way!"
While yet he spake, and looked

      around with a bewildered stare,
Four sturdy lictors put their necks

      beneath the curule chair;
And fourscore clients on the left,

      and fourscore on the right,
Arrayed themselves with swords and staves,

      and loins girt up for fight.
But, though without or staff or sword,

      so furious was the throng,
That scarce the train with might

      and main could bring their lord along.

Twelve times the crowd made at him;
        five times they seized his gown;
Small chance was his to rise again,
        if once they got him down:
And sharper came the pelting;
        and evermore the yell—
"Tribunes! we will have tribunes!"—
        rose with a louder swell:
And the chair tossed as tosses
        a bark with tattered sail
When raves the Adriatic
        beneath an Eastern gale,
When the Calabrian sea-marks
        are lost in clouds of spume,
And the great Thunder-Cape
        has donned his veil of inky gloom.
One stone hit Appius in the mouth,
        and one beneath the ear;
And ere he reached Mount Palatine,
        he swooned with pain and fear.

His cursèd head, that he was wont
   to hold so high with pride,
Now, like a drunken man's, hung down,
   and swayed from side to side;
And when his stout retainers
   had brought him to his door,
His face and neck were all one cake
   of filth and clotted gore.
As Appius Claudius was that day,
   so may his grandson be!
God send Rome one such other sight,
   and send me there to see!

THE PROPHECY OF CAPYS

A LAY SUNG AT THE BANQUET IN THE CAPI-
TOL, ON THE DAY WHEREON MANIUS CURIUS
DENTATUS, A SECOND TIME CONSUL, TRIUMPHED
OVER KING PYRRHUS AND THE TARENTINES
IN THE YEAR OF THE CITY CCCCLXXIX.

I.

NOW slain is King Amulius,
 Of the great Sylvian line,
Who reigned in Alba Longa,
 On the throne of Aventine.
Slain is the Pontiff Camers,
 Who spake the words of doom:
"The children to the Tiber;
 The mother to the tomb."

II.

In Alba's lake no fisher
  His net to-day is flinging:
On the dark rind of Alba's oaks
  To-day no axe is ringing:
The yoke hangs o'er the manger:
  The scythe lies in the hay:
Through all the Alban villages
  No work is done to-day.

III.

And every Alban burgher
  Hath donned his whitest gown:
And every head in Alba
  Weareth a poplar crown:
And every Alban door-post
  With boughs and flowers is gay:
For to-day the dead are living:
  The lost are found to-day.

IV.

They were doomed
                by a bloody king:
They were doomed
                by a lying priest:
They were cast on the raging flood:
They were tracked
                by the raging beast:
Raging beast and raging flood
    Alike have spared the prey;
And to-day the dead are living:
    The lost are found to-day.

V.

The troubled river knew them,
    And smoothed his yellow foam,
And gently rocked the cradle
    That bore the fate of Rome.
The ravening she-wolf knew them,
    And licked them o'er and o'er,
And gave them of her own fierce milk
    Rich with raw flesh and gore.

Marching from Alba Longa
To their old grandsires' hall.

Twenty winters, twenty springs,
  Since then have rolled away:
And to-day the dead are living:
  The lost are found to-day.

VI.

Blithe it was to see the twins,
  Right goodly youths and tall,
Marching from Alba Longa
  To their old grandsire's hall.
Along their path fresh garlands
  Are hung from tree to tree:
Before them stride the pipers,
  Piping a note of glee.

VII.

On the right goes Romulus,
  With arms to the elbows red,
And in his hand a broadsword,
  And on the blade a head —

A head in an iron helmet,
　　With horsehair hanging down,
A shaggy head, a swarthy head,
　　Fixed in a ghastly frown—
The head of King Amulius,
　　Of the great Sylvian line,
Who reigned in Alba Longa,
　　On the throne of Aventine.

VIII.

On the left side goes Remus,
　　With wrists and fingers red,
And in his hand a boar-spear,
　　And on the point a head—
A wrinkled head and aged,
　　With silver beard and hair.
And holy fillets round it,
　　Such as the pontiffs wear—
The head of ancient Camers,
　　Who spake the words of doom:

"The children to the Tiber;
The mother to the tomb."

IX.

Two and two behind the twins
Their trusty comrades go,
Four and forty valiant men,
With club, and axe, and bow.
On each side every hamlet
Pours forth its joyous crowd,
Shouting lads and baying dogs
And children laughing loud,
And old men weeping fondly
As Rhea's boys go by,
And maids who shriek
to see the heads,
Yet, shrieking, press more nigh.

X.

So they marched along the lake;
They marched by fold and stall,

By corn-field and by vineyard,
    Unto the old man's hall.

XI.

In the hall-gate sate Capys,
    Capys, the sightless seer:
From head to foot he trembled
    As Romulus drew near.

And up stood stiff his thin white hair
  And his blind eyes flashed fire:
"Hail! foster child
          of the wondrous nurse!
Hail! son of the wondrous sire!

XII.

"But thou—what dost thou here
  In the old man's peaceful hall?
What doth the eagle in the coop,
  The bison in the stall?
Our corn fills many a garner;
  Our vines clasp many a tree;
Our flocks are white on many a hill,
  But these are not for thee.

XIII.

"For thee no treasure ripens
  In the Tartessian mine:
For thee no ship brings precious bales
  Across the Libyan brine:

Thou shalt not drink from amber;
  Thou shalt not rest on down;
Arabia shall not steep thy locks,
  Nor Sidon tinge thy gown.

XIV.

"Leave gold and myrrh and jewels,
  Rich table and soft bed,
To them who of man's seed are born,
  Whom woman's milk hath fed.
Thou wast not made for lucre,
  For pleasure, nor for rest:
Thou, that are sprung
        from the War-god's loins,
  And hast tugged
        at the she-wolf's breast.

XV.

"From sunrise unto sunset
  All earth shall hear thy fame:
A glorious city thou shalt build,
  And name it by thy name:

And there, unquenched through ages,
    Like Vesta's sacred fire,
Shall live the spirit of thy nurse,
    The spirit of thy sire.

XVI.

"The ox toils through the furrow,
    Obedient to the goad;
The patient ass, up flinty paths,
    Plods with his weary load;
With whine and bound the spaniel
    His master's whistle hears;
And the sheep yields her patiently
    To the loud clashing shears.

XVII.

"But thy nurse will hear no master;
    Thy nurse will bear no load;
And woe to them that shear her,
    And woe to them that goad!

When all the pack, loud baying,
  Her bloody lair surrounds,
She dies in silence, biting hard,
  Amidst the dying hounds.

XVIII.

"Pomona loves the orchard;
  And Liber loves the vine;
And Pales loves the straw-built shed
  Warm with the breath of kine;
And Venus loves the whispers
  Of plighted youth and maid,
In April's ivory moonlight
  Beneath the chestnut shade.

XIX.

"But thy father loves the clashing
  Of broadsword and of shield:
He loves to drink the steam that reeks
  From the fresh battle-field;

He smiles a smile more dreadful
Than his own dreadful frown,
When he sees the thick
   black cloud of smoke
Go up from the conquered town.

XX.

"And such as is the War-god,
The author of thy line,

And such as she who suckled thee,
    Even such be thou and thine.
Leave to the soft Campanian
    His baths and his perfumes;
Leave to the sordid race of Tyre
    Their dyeing-vats and looms:
Leave to the sons of Carthage
    The rudder and the oar:
Leave to the Greek
            his marble Nymphs
    And scrolls of wordy lore.

XXI.

"Thine, Roman, is the pilum:
    Roman, the sword is thine,
The even trench, the bristling mound,
    The legion's ordered line;
And thine the wheels of triumph,
    Which with their laurelled train
Move slowly up the shouting streets
    To Jove's eternal fane.

XXII.

"Beneath thy yoke the Volscian
  Shall vail his lofty brow:
Soft Capua's curled revellers
  Before thy chairs shall bow:
The Lucumoes of Arnus
  Shall quake thy rods to see;
And the proud Samnite's
                heart of steel
  Shall yield to only thee.

XXIII.

"The Gaul shall come against thee
From the land of snow and night:
Thou shalt give his fair-haired armies
To the raven and the kite.

XXIV.

"The Greek shall come against thee,
The conqueror of the East.
Beside him stalks to battle
The huge earth-shaking beast,
The beast on whom the castle
With all its guards doth stand,
The beast who hath between his eyes
The serpent for a hand.
First march the bold Epirotes,
Wedged close
                with shield and spear;
And the ranks of false Tarentum
Are glittering in the rear.

XXV.

"The ranks of false Tarentum
  Like hunted sheep shall fly:
In vain the bold Epirotes
  Shall round their standards die:
And Apennine's grey vultures
  Shall have a noble feast
On the fat and the eyes
  Of the huge earth-shaking beast.

XXVI.

"Hurrah! for the good weapons
  That keep the War-god's land.
Hurrah! for Rome's stout pilum
  In a stout Roman hand.
Hurrah! for Rome's short broadsword,
  That through the thick array
Of levelled spears and serried shields
  Hews deep its gory way.

XXVII.

"Hurrah! for the great triumph
That stretches many a mile.
Hurrah! for the wan captives
That pass in endless file.

Ho! bold Epirotes, whither
    Hath the Red King ta'en flight?
Ho! dogs of false Tarentum,
    Is not the gown washed white?

XXVIII.

"Hurrah! for the great triumph
That stretches many a mile.
Hurrah! for the rich dye of Tyre,
And the fine web of Nile,
The helmets gay with plumage
Torn from the pheasant's wings,
The belts set thick with starry gems
That shone on Indian kings,
The urns of massy silver,
The goblets rough with gold,
The many-coloured tablets bright
With loves and wars of old,
The stone that breathes and struggles,
The brass that seems to speak;—
Such cunning they who dwell on high
Have given unto the Greek.

XXIX.

"Hurrah! for Manius Curius,
  The bravest son of Rome,
Thrice in utmost need sent forth,
  Thrice drawn in triumph home.
Weave, weave, for Manius Curius
  The third embroidered gown:
Make ready the third lofty car,
  And twine the third green crown;
And yoke the steeds of Rosea
  With necks like a bended bow,
And deck the bull, Mevania's bull,
  The bull as white as snow.

XXX.

"Blest and thrice blest the Roman
    Who sees Rome's brightest day,
Who sees that long victorious pomp
    Wind down the Sacred Way,
And through the bellowing Forum,
    And round the Suppliant's Grove,
Up to the everlasting gates
    Of Capitolian Jove.

XXXI.

"Then where, o'er two bright havens
    The towers of Corinth frown;
Where the gigantic King of Day
    On his own Rhodes looks down;
Where soft Orontes murmurs
    Beneath the laurel shades;
Where Nile reflects the endless length
    Of dark-red colonnades;
Where in the still deep water,
    Sheltered from waves and blasts,

Bristles the dusky forest
   Of Byrsa's thousand masts;
Where fur-clad hunters wander
   Amidst the northern ice;
Where through the sand
            of morning-land
   The camel bears the spice;
Where Atlas flings his shadow
   Far o'er the western foam,
Shall be great fear on all who hear
   The mighty name of Rome."

Printed in Bavaria.